W9-CQY-083

Published 1986 by Derrydale Books,
distributed by Crown Publishers, Inc.

Produced for Derrydale Books by
Victoria House Publishing Ltd.
4/5 Lower Borough Walls
Bath BA1 1QR, England

Printed in Singapore

Someone
To Play With

Illustrated by Stephen Cartwright
Written by Jean Kenward

Derrydale Books
New York

Here's my Dad! He's carrying a huge, huge paper bag. It is a present for me.

What is in the bag? It is not a pencil . . .
or a banana . . . It feels like a BALL.

It IS! The ball is green, blue, and red.
I can see a yellow piece, too.

I roll the ball over the floor. I roll it slowly.
I roll it *fast*.

THUMP! The ball bumps into Mommy's legs.
Mommy is making the dinner.

"Take that ball away!"
she cries. "Play outside!"

My Dad says he will play with me. We put
on our ski hats. We put on our jogging suits.

We put on our boots. We go outside.

There is some great mud in a puddle. I roll
the ball in the mud. Squash!

My Dad throws the ball to me. I get mud
on my jogging suit. I get mud on my chin.

My Dad likes to play football. He gives the
ball a small kick. He gives it a big, big kick.

The ball flies up in the air. It goes next door.
It is gone.

We can hear someone next door. My Dad
calls out "Can we have our ball back, please?"
The ball comes over the fence all by itself!

The fence has a little hole in it, as high
as my nose. I peep through the hole. The girl
next door peeps through the hole, too.

"We can be friends!" she says. "We can play ball together! I'll come over."

AND SHE DOES.